This Book Belongs To

. . . .

Space Dog

Goes to Planet Purrgo

Vivian French

Illustrated by Sue Heap

Hodder
Children's
Books

A division of Hodder Headline Limited

To Alice

CHAPTER ONE

It was the middle of the day.
Space Dog was busy ironing.

Blue Moon, Green Moon
and Purple Moon
were fast asleep.

Big Sun was shining happily.

Little Sun was skipping with three tube worms.

"Space Dog!" he called.
"Will you come and skip with me?"
Space Dog popped out of his Kennel.

"Sorry, Little Sun," he said.
"I can't skip now. I'm packing."

"Where are you going?" asked Little Sun.
"I'm off to visit Space Cat!" said Space Dog

Little Sun jumped up and down.
"Can I come, too?"

"Sorry!" said Space Dog. "Not this time—"

It was the bone phone.

Space Dog picked it up.

"Space Cat?" said Space Dog. "Are you all right?"

"No!" Space Cat howled."My planet is running away! Come quickly! I need help!"

Space Dog grabbed his suitcase.
"Say goodbye to everyone for me," he
shouted, as he whizzed past Big Sun.
"I've got to fly! Bye!"

Big Sun waved. "Oh! Have you seen
Little Sun?—"

Space Dog did not answer. He was
busy zooming off towards Planet
Purrgo.

On and on Space Dog flew. Through
Inner Space and Outer Space.
There was no Planet Purrgo to be
seen.

"Hmmm," he thought. "How odd.
Where can it have got to?"

"COOOEEE! SPACE DOG!"
Space Dog stopped in mid-air.

"That sounds like Star Rock Four,"
he said.

"BOO!"
said Star
Rock Four.
She blew a
cloud out
of the
way.

"Hello, Star Rock Four!" said Space Dog, as he landed. "I'm looking for Planet Purrgo. Have you seen it?"

Star Rock Four nodded and pointed down. "Saw it I did that way going."

"Bother," said Space Dog. "The chills
are down there. It's so COLD—
Hey! Everything's wobbling!"

He clutched at his suitcase.
"Whatever's going on?"
Star Rock Four was wriggling all over.
"Phew!" she said. "HOT I am, and
NOISE I hear. SQUEAKINGS!"

"OH NO!" said Space Dog, and he
opened his suitcase.
Inside was Little Sun, and three
BOILING tube worms.

"Hello, Space Dog," said Little Sun.
"Is this Planet Purrgo?"

"Little Sun!" Space Dog scratched his head. "You CAN'T come with me! Whatever will I do with you?!"

"BOO HOO HOO!"

Little Sun burst into tears.

"Ahem," Star Rock
Four coughed politely.
"Idea I have.
Worms like rope are.
Pull suitcase with
worms?"

Space Dog heaved a huge sigh.
He tied the worms around his waist.
"All right," he said. "Let's go."

"Luck much to you!" said Star Rock Four, waving goodbye.

Space Dog nodded. "We'll need it," he said. Then he whizzed away.

"WHEEE!" yelled Little Sun.

Behind them Star Rock Four stopped waving.

"Oh NO!" she said. "Never did I say to watch out for Woopers! SILLY me!"

Behind her back, a little swarm of Woopers giggled. "TICKLY TICKLY TICKLY! WOOP WOOP WOOP!"

CHAPTER TWO

Space Dog flew on. "Brrr! It's getting cold," he muttered.
The tube worms were looking anxious. They were beginning to

stre-e-e-e-e-tch.
"Woof! There it is!"
Space Dog barked a happy bark,
and began to dive.

"MEEOW! MEEOW! ATCHOO!"
Space Cat was perched on a tree.
The only tree on Planet Purrgo.

A group of Threepies were huddled
beside her. They looked very cold
and miserable.

"Good afternoon, Space Cat," said Space Dog, as he landed with a thump.

Little Sun bounced up and down. The tube worms shivered and curled up into a knot.

"SPACE DOG!" Space Cat leapt from
her tree. "I'm so pleased to see you . . .

Oh! You've brought me Little Sun!" She
held out her paws to warm them.
Little Sun beamed and beamed.

"Er . . . yes," said Space Dog. "Now, what are we going to do about this planet of yours?"

Space Cat sneezed again.
"It just won't settle anywhere," she said. "If ONLY it would find a place in space it liked. It will keep running away to somewhere else—"

Planet Purrgo gave a sudden twitch.
Space Cat clutched at Space Dog.
Space Dog clutched at Little Sun.

The Threepies fell out of the tree, and
landed on top of the tube worms.

"I think Planet Purrgo wants to tell us something," said Space Dog.
The little planet twitched again, and then it spoke, in a tiny, dusty voice.

"But I'M your friend," said Space Cat.

Space Dog clapped his paws.

"Easy!" he said. "Come home with me! Purrgo can chat to Blue Moon and Green Moon, and Purple Moon. Big Sun will keep her warm!"

Space Cat began to purr. "PURRfect! PURRfect!"

"I'll show you the way," Space Dog told Purrgo. "Just zoom up after me!"
"Can't," whispered Purrgo.

Too cold to zoom

Space Dog rubbed his nose.

Space Cat stopped purring.

"I know!" said Little Sun. "Space Dog can tow us home!"

The tube worms
were not happy.
They did not want
to be ropes again.

"PLEASE!" purred Space Cat.
"PRETTY please!"
"For me?" tried Space Dog, in his
nicest voice.

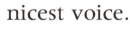

"You can
swing on
my swing!"
said Little
Sun.

At last the tube worms agreed.
Space Cat, the Threepies and Little
Sun held tightly to the tree.

Space Dog and the worms got ready.
"ONE! TWO! THREE! GO!" shouted
Space Dog -

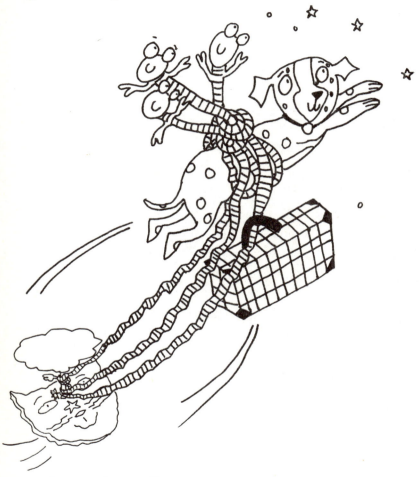

and up they flew . . .

"TICKLY! TICKLY TICKLY! WOOP
WOOP WOOP!"
Behind them zoomed a swarm of
Woopers.

They dived straight into the the tube
worms.

"EEEK!" squeaked the worms, and
they let go of Space Dog.
Planet Purrgo began to fall . . .
DOWN and DOWN . . .

but Space Dog was ready.
With a mighty WHOOOSH! he
grabbed the suitcase . . .

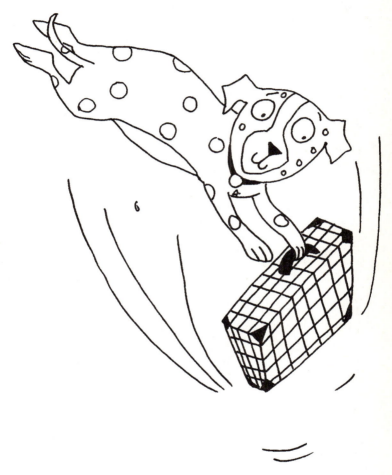

. . . and got ready to open it wide . . .

He SWOOOPED down to the buzzing
Woopers, scooped them all up . . . and

BANG! He shut the suitcase lid . . .

and threw the case down towards
the Chills.

"WOOF!"
Space Dog double-flipped . . .
swung back to
Purrgo . . .

and stared.

CHAPTER THREE

Planet Purrgo wasn't falling any more.
She was floating . . . slowly . . . and
steadily . . . upwards.

"You can! You can!" shouted Space
Dog and Space Cat.

Little Sun shone as
hard as he could.

It was a very long journey.
Space Dog pushed Purrgo from
underneath.

Little Sun, Space Cat and the
Threepies sang helpful songs.

The tube worms waved their tails in time.

CHAPTER FOUR

At long last . . . they were home.

"LITTLE SUN!"
Big Sun was shining down above
them. He glared at Little Sun.

"Where have you been!?"

Little Sun simply beamed.

"Space Dog will explain!" he said.

Space Dog smiled. "He's been helping me rescue Planet Purggo, Big Sun . . . We couldn't have done it without him!"

Big Sun hugged Little Sun.

Space Cat and Space Dog sat down on
Planet Purrgo.

And the Threepies and the tube
worms cheered . . . and cheered . . .
and cheered .